This Little Tiger book belongs to:

_____

_____

_____

_____

For Mum
~MC

For Cassie
~VC

LITTLE TIGER PRESS
An imprint of Magi Publications
1 The Coda Centre, 189 Munster Road, London SW6 6AW, UK
www.littletigerpress.com

First published in Great Britain 2002
by Little Tiger Press, London
This edition published in 2008

ISBN 978-1-84506-886-8

Printed in China

2 4 6 8 10 9 7 5 3 1

Where There's A Bear, There's TROUBLE!

Michael Catchpool & Vanessa Cabban

LITTLE TIGER PRESS

One brown bear saw one yellow bee. And one yellow bee saw one brown bear.

One brown bear thought, "Where there's a bee there's honey . . . sticky honey, yummy honey, drippy honey, gummy honey. I'll follow this bee as quietly as can be."

One yellow bee thought, "Where there's
a bear there's trouble. I'll buzz off home
as quickly as can be."

So one yellow bee buzzed off over the
stone wall . . .

followed by one brown bear,
as quietly as could be on his
softest tip-toes.

Buzz! Buzz! Growl! Growl! Shh!

Two greedy geese spotted one tip-toeing bear.
"Ah-ha," they thought. "Where there's a bear
there are berries . . . ripe berries, juicy berries,
plump berries, squishy berries. Let's follow that
bear as quietly as can be."

So two greedy geese followed
one brown bear, and one brown
bear followed one yellow bee . . .

Buzz! Buzz! Growl! Growl! Honk! Honk! Shh!

all going along as quietly as can be.

Three shy mice spied two flapping geese.
"Ah-ha," they thought, "where there are
geese, there's corn . . .

yellow corn, yummy corn, delicious corn, tasty corn. Let's follow those geese as quietly as can be."

Buzz! Buzz! Growl! Growl! Honk! Honk! Squeak.

So one yellow bee buzzed over the bramble bush, and one brown bear followed one yellow bee, and two greedy geese followed one brown bear, and three shy mice followed two greedy geese, all going along as quietly as could be!

Then one yellow bee buzzed right into its nest . . .

Squeak! Shh!

and one hundred yellow
bees buzzed out!

One brown bear saw one hundred yellow bees, and one hundred yellow bees saw one brown bear.

"HELP!" growled one brown bear. "Where there's a swarm there must be

TROUBLE!

I'll run back home as quickly as can be!"

And off he raced, back through the prickly bramble bush.

"Help!" squawked the two greedy geese. "The bear is after us!" And off they flapped across the muddy field.

"Help!" squeaked the three shy mice. "The geese are after us!" And off they scrambled through a crack in the stone wall, until . . .

Growl! Ouch!

Squawk! Hiss!

Squeak! Eek!

CRASH!

One yellow bee landed on one brown bear, and one brown bear landed on two greedy geese, and two greedy geese landed on three shy mice.

And one yellow bee thought, "I knew there'd be trouble!"

Fantastic reads from Little Tiger Press

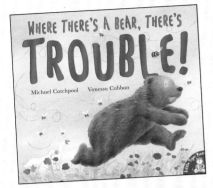

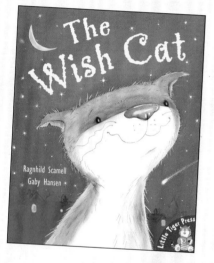

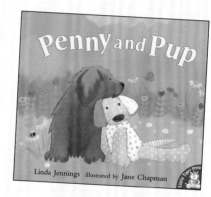

For information regarding any of the above titles
or for our catalogue, please contact us:
Little Tiger Press, 1 The Coda Centre,
189 Munster Road, London SW6 6AW, UK
Tel: +44 (0)20 7385 6333 Fax: +44 (0)20 7385 7333
E-mail: info@littletiger.co.uk
www.littletigerpress.com